I0758435

The Glory of Sunflowers

Book III
A town Unknown

Amatielle

ISBN 978-1-956001-63-1 (paperback)
ISBN 978-1-956001-64-8 (eBook)

Copyright © 2021 by Amatielle

All rights reserved. No part of this publication may be reproduced, distributed, or transmitted in any form or by any means, including photocopying, recording, or other electronic or mechanical methods without the prior written permission of the publisher.

Printed in the United States of America

Tajane held on. She was deeply in love, she was Enmeshed, engorged, entrenched in an intricate web of conjugal lust, and, expensive calls. Shank wasn't the only one paying for his past mistake of nearly taking a young man's life in his fake friend's robbery.

Tajane was like him. She only nineteen but was a prisoner just like Shank. He was tall with dark hair, fair skinned with a natural tan like his mother bore an Italian, he had tattoos on his arms, back, and chest, and white boy dreadlocks. Really he was the blackest white dude she had ever dated.

But this wasn't dating. This was awaiting a parole date. Sway was certain his daughter would make better choices but she didn't on this one.

Charity had three miscarriages on the way to Tajane.

She began to hate life, God, all creation and stopped watching television and movies all together.

She bought and collected exotically realistic doll babies, dressed them and had an entire room in their home they called the nursery. At first it creeped Sway out, but he caved to his wife's emotional needs as the room filled with real baby accessories. Charity made her own money at the library, and she was free to spend it how she chose. Sway was a largely successful financial advisor with his own firm now.

People often confused him for an attorney or accountant, but he was just a young man with a passion for helping his people heal from poverty, and that is what drove him.

He funded a small chain of a company called The Money Doctor from Southwest Atlanta to North West Georgia and now in several other states. They had money, but better than that they had love.

People of all kinds went there. Some had no money, and some had plenty, but it was a system that worked, and he had been on the Today show in New York, Money Live, Stirred up all kinds of controversy, and President Donald J.

Trump showed up at his office on Peachtree and 14th Street with President Barak Obama and a photographer took all kinds of pictures for People Magazine, Forbes, Black Enterprise, Upscale, Rolling Out, Creative Loafing, Everyone covered the story, even publications that didn't cover stories covered the story. He was a big deal, and many wanted him to run for mayor, but he wouldn't.

Sway and Charity were straight after that.

Money had never been a problem for them.

Sway finally sold his grandmother's home with an increase of forty percent in the property value after enhancements and redoing the downstairs bathroom. He bought some land in the center of town and put up a custom home for the two of them- hobbies and all and that was home for them. Life was good. It had been over twenty years. Where had time gone so quickly?

Charity lay still in the bed that morning. She couldn't force herself up to look in the mirror and feel her belly again. It was different every time, and every time she wanted her babies.

They stopped. Heartbeat's never seemed to start, or never seemed to start and stay.

She lost her mind on the first one. Her body was cold to her and her mind was dark and ashy grey. Life went from color to black and white and periods were a painful reminder of failed dreams.

Sway refused to adopt. He wanted to build a 'true' legacy and since Charity was adopted and raised by her aunt she had a debt of gratitude, after all her aunt went through to make ways for her in life. Sway and Charity were very attractive people and he wanted to have some good looking babies with her or none at all.

Sway was a good looking in more ways than one. It had been damned difficult to remain faithful, true, monogamous and loyal to his wife in the city of Atlanta for the first two years of married life, and opportunities came frequently and close together for this near fortune five black man who stayed in the gym regularly.

Charity had plenty options, she was beautiful.

Her long hair careened down her back, and was a fabulous full curly afro when she wanted.

Charity set trends with every step. So much so that she had to be mindful of where she went, who she spoke to, what she bought, where she bought it from, what she read, watched, and so forth. Her style was a contagious thing to women everywhere, and she felt no glory. All she wanted was the gift of a living, breathing, beautiful child of her own with her husband.

She was forty three then.

Sway was gone to work that morning. This time (the second time) Charity lay in bed and thought about driving all the way to Savannah straight into the sea.

Each time she had these thoughts that seemed to pull her like a magnet she saw her husband.

Young, holding her hand in his, kissing her forehead, caressing her thighs, kissing her back, calling out her name from the other end of the house, standing there in the shower with her.

It would be goodbye to those things. It would be goodbye to eating foods they never thought they would or could at restaurants, and countries they never thought they would go.

The wildly vivid feeling of making U-turns in a foreign land, where the people, places and things were so much the same but so much different at the same time. They had been to Thailand, Madrid, Curtiba, Rio, Peru, Mazatlan, Upstate NY, Denver, Seattle, Houston, London, Paris, and Amsterdam. Charity's life with him was a myriad of adventure and she stopped feeling it all this day, the day she lost her second pregnancy.

It was a regularly scheduled doctor visit in trimester one. Sway was there as always. He busted his ass working to make sure he could afford the life and time he made for his wife and he did well.

Charity lay on the noisy white paper on the padded table beneath her.

She was uncomfortable and felt that something was wrong.

Sway held her hand standing opposite the Radiologist whose face had gone piqued.

There was the longest silence in the world, in that room.

Sway looked at the technician after thirty minutes of ear shattering quiet had passed by feeling like hours.

Charity lay there with the now cooled jelly on her abdomen and a rolling, searching sonar device being hand manipulated by the woman who was young, blonde, and explained that she had to put her little dog down that morning.

Sharee put the device back in its holder.

Charity would have been fifteen weeks along.

Share clasped her hands and she said to Charity, "There is no heartbeat. I'm sorry"

Charity froze there on the table, it was like invisible ice engulfed her body from her toes to her hairline. Concrete.

She was a casket again. Sway was silent and a tear rolled out of his right eye and on to Charity's forehead as he was cradling her head now.

"Has this happened before?" the technician gently spurted out.

The two of them shook their heads in acknowledgement.

The pain in the room was tangible. It was big and looming all around Charity and that is when she began to be different than she was before.

"We will try again baby, we will try again.

God's got it, got it got it." Sway said as he held Charity in his arms through her guilt which seemed to bore a hole in her soul in this moment.

"It's my fault?" She asked through tears of the most evil sorrow while her being seemed somehow to be quick sanded away from the world in slow motion.

Sway had the best psychiatric care lined up for her at Well Again.

They had support from friends and family but Charity was effected and didn't budge from the change for a year, and the last time they agreed to stop and put it out of their minds, all of it.

There were fights. Arguments about nothing with a bit of blame tucked carefully with in the core.

Their life drug on like that for one more year.

There were lots of trips, and lots of around town outings, business awards, and functions, causes to fund, and the dolls. Charity began an expensive and beautiful doll collection of Reborn baby dolls with cribs, strollers, diapers, and all of the trimmings they had from their pregnancy rollercoasters. It was cathartic and healing for Charity and she bought and sold dolls this way on E-bay, Amazon, and websites dedicated solely to the cause of doll therapy.

She had friends in the community and the light started to seep back into her slowly.

Charity and Sway were more mature now.

Just four years and a day apart and perfect soulmates. They learned to grow through their pain and mistakes and had truly perfected their love together as people.

March was always a fabulous month for them.

These tiny creations from Natali Blick and her many muses the amazing doll artists around the world were like a healing bouquet to Charity's soul.

Charity had put on weight in her midsection.

Her cycle was irregular and she graciously believed she was in menopause or some change due to her so called age.

She was fabulous and fit, and acting out her life as if one or two her doll babies were real and she held that picture in her mind like sunrays and that and moving her body in the gym and dance class even through the grey concrete of depression made a slow, painful though steady and hopeful existence her own.

Sway's heart broke for his wife, and he thrust his focus, passion, and pain into his work.

He would give her everything he could if not to heal her then to quell her pain, and this did his also.

Charity felt old. She wasn't at all, just a late mother.

She lay in bed that morning after collecting memories and dusting them off, the morning light pouring in through the window…She had stopped having her period for almost half a year now.

The 'change of life' was upon her. She began to have acceptance for her healing where there used to be a cold, dull, lifeless, hard ache.

There was pain on the fourteenth of February.

She thought certainly she was dying.

Sway had a car rush them to the emergency room as he sat with her in the back doing grounding exercises the therapists had taught them over the months and days which had passed, helping her through the abdominal pain and panicky.

They got to the emergency room, they drew blood and next thing you know she was in the maternity ward.

Then Tajine. The pain seemed to subside as soon as it began, and Charity felt the spirit of God with in her speaking, saying ; I Am, and then the most beautiful, healthy ten fingered, ten toes baby slid gently from her womb into their lives and every bit of sorrow and former dullness was gone. Just like that. She was a silent miracle who crept up on them in the darkest emotional despair. They had everything materially, home, cars, investments, organizations for whatever they cared to contribute to… but the absence of their child was a void, ever growing which had not stopped until Charity named the babies she lost. She made memoriam and reconciliation in her heart, and moved on with these doll babies as a hobby, and prayed through it. God's love was all over them.

They had been finessed in his favor and Tajane was the love of their lives. An only child, but a miraculous gift to her parents.

That was nineteen years ago and her best dream come true ever. Tajane was truly the glory of sunflowers in the garden of her mother and father's heart and Sway said as much when he first lay eyes on his beautiful baby girl. Growing up for Tajane was good. The family travelled together, but her role was well defined.

Her parents were themselves much like one person rather than two, and she was herself but still one of them. The three of them were not only husband and wife, mother, and father, and child, but a unit, and Tajane was a well behaved child.

She was aware of her parents struggle before her and she sought to give them the most ideal experience a child could. Their struggle matured her and caused her to be more humane and considerate than children her age. They raised her in church. She saw miracles, the power of prayer, hypocracy at its finest, and the beauty of forgiveness right in front of her.

Mrs. Cathers was hit by a car while walking through a busy intersection, it killed her grandson as the bumper of his Nissan swept the two out of the way and the baby and stroller crushed into a nearby telephone pole. The baby was intact on the outside but died soon after from head trauma and Mrs. Cathers and deacon Cathers were devastated. Their son had been incarcerated for drug trafficking before the tiny boy was born and low and behold if she didn't bring that man's entire family to church three years later.

That was surely the grace of God. Then there was Mr. Bryant. He was an old creep of a pedophile of a man no one wanted to be alone with where avoidable.

He was quiet and then transparent with artificial jovial superficial chirp the next.

Tajine's best friend Munier was molested by him in the second grade.

Kajika and her brother Victor were also his suspected Sunday school victims. They were foster kids.

For a while no one knew accept the two girls, but one sleep over they made a promise to each other to take a stand.

Tajane knew her little friend was telling the truth because the horrible things she described couldn't even have come out of a movie, and he had a smell, and she talked about that and his cat's chopped off tail, though he only had a dog and for the life of anyone there was no reason at all little Munier would have had to go in this man's house and see his dirty ass scruffy dog.

Besides looking at a funny looking and neglected animal and had nothing to do with him pulling down her nine year old friend's underwear or him taking his thing out and telling her people go to hell for telling secrets. It took a detestable two Sundays and Rev. Rainey's sermon on lie and how not telling the truth was the same as lying and how people even lie to themselves. The girls looked at eachother standing there in the children's choir after the selection in the middle of the service. They had an instant knowing. They were telling on Mr. Bryant's funny smelling ass.

The police went to Mrs. Thomas's house at 5:45pm after service that same Sunday and that man went to jail on two counts of sexual assault of a minor.

He was gone a very long time, and then when the girls turned seventeen, there he was, like nothing ever happened. They felt free.

Upon his prison return he apologized openly to the church, and some scoffed at him. Others grew pale and silent.

There were meetings about it, and special prayer, and everything went back to normal again but this time he was a known threat rather than a dark secret.

Time served. Rev. Rainey's church was not a small congregation. He was a pastor not quite big enough to be accused of heinous conspiracy and perversion, but it was common knowledge that he had sex offenders, drug dealers, ex-convicts, adulterers, and good old fashioned liars in his congregation and his church quickly got the nick name 'the forgiveness church' in many church circles.

The pastor was a loving, kind, strong, honest, and forgiving man and he required no less from his congregation.

And many were delivered at his services.

Sometimes he would get a word from God about a person in dire need and he would take a love offering up and ask them to come forward. They would go home with whatever it yielded and Rev.

Rainey, now nearly seventy six would declare and thank God for the perfect amount needed.

Stranger's bills got paid at service all the time, from rent to groceries, and the church grew bigger and fast.

People came back and testified about their car's being spared from repossession, medicine that saved the day, eviction being stopped dead in it's tracks, one lady was able to get a nebulizer for her daughter and then God healed the girl of Asthma and COPD. God had blessed them to be able to move into a newer home with a better ventilation system and the lady quit smoking and which was also a miracle of sorts.

Because of these awesome things happening in life which she witnessed forever, she had strong faith in God and the church, and seemed jaded although she was not.

Summers were full of retreats, wedding anniversary celebrations, youth fitness camps, deliverance expos, and church revival events. There was food, young musicians and actors retreats and family, gospel music and good preaching.

Tajane wanted something.

She wanted something like the glow her parents got when each of the other one walked in the room. She was lonely as an only child, and though they always explained to her the long arduous journey they made for her to be born, and how we are all brothers and sisters in Christ, and how family is what we make it…she began to yearn for this thing of television, and teen Romance novels, her parent's looks at each other, and Munier had a boyfriend now.

At least for what a seventeen year old could call a boyfriend. She and Roy had known each other since the fourth grade, and that was just the most romantic thing anyone had ever heard of. It was like they were destined to be together and then at sixteen he kissed her at the Black Panther the movie and that was it.

They were booed up.

Munier said Roy's kiss tasted like watermelon jolly ranchers.

Tajane was naturally jealous at having to share her best friend, but they survived it. After all Munier had a debt of gratitude towards Tajane because her friend gave her the courage to tell on her sexual predator. This kept her self-worth intact which was something no one could say about Mr. Bryant's other sorted and unknown victims in the community.

Prospects looked slim to Tajane. She was a confident girl, and certainly had the looks and brains to back it up. There were only four boys her age at church two of them Black like her, one Asian and one Latino but in her eyes all of them ordinary.

Caprice was the nerdy one. He was a scrawny little dude with an ordinary haircut and some high water pants.

Jordan was the Spanish one, the cuter one with light green eyes and some muscles for his young age.

His parents were assistant pastors and he had a creased attitude at church and seemed to hunt girls at school.

Mostly the girls in class tried to avoid him because he would make you kiss him or creep up and breathe on your neck behind your open lockers door without your permission if you let him.

Chance was handsome. Quiet. Polite but always

Where ever his mother was in a shy kind of way, And the Eli was the Black and Asian one who was always getting in trouble with his teachers for talking but he could sing really well and always got solos at church.

He said when he grew up he was going to take a girl on a date in the woods…

Jody was a tomboy girl who would pretend to follow around Munier and Tajane between classes, but she played a lot of sports so that never lasted long.

She got with Tracy by the end of Summer ninth grade and they were serious and inseparable.

Trey was closet gay and super popular, and he didn't have a boyfriend but he was an entertainingly comical kid with braces and he flirt with everybody male or female like it was his job.

He was pretty with light brown eyes brown skin and curly eyelashes.

He used to go with Tajane the year before but she denied him because he was so lispy and broken wristed. He made a much better girlfriend so by the end of Senior year, that's where they kept it.

Someone later told her Trey was on Facebook with his new look in black plastic leather and a slew of community friends who were team Pride, so Tajane just forgive his dishonesty and blatant denial of homosexuality as him being him but she never looked back.

He wanted her to have his baby, and she wasn't yet even supposed to be having sex so it didn't work, they grew apart.

This experience made Tajane believe that any man could be gay if he wanted to, and that they were easy liars, so she never expected much, and therefore became shelled in to protect herself.

Only her father Sway was good, and he seemed to be the last of a dying breed.

Tajine's high school graduation was magical.

She felt such a sigh of relief and calm, excitement and anticipation as if the world would be handed to her with that diploma. Soon after ward, she sat in her seat recapping the moment.

"Tajine McDaniel's A P Honors" and she tossed up her cap early and then gathered it for the ending. She kicked Biology's ass after all.

Sway sent her and Munier to Paris and she was awarded a white Mercedes Benz 350 SUV with tan leather interior just like her mother's accept her's said *Tajine* on the front, and her personalized plates said TAJ1

Her mother's said Charity on the front and her tag said WIFI3K on it.

The kids teased Charity saying it looked like she was saying she was Sway's three thousandth wife or that she was three thousand years old.

It was just the regular running family joke or two reminding everyone they were at home with eachother.

Both Charity and Sway hollered loud when their almost grown up baby girl walked the stage and it was a beautiful and unforgettable moment, complete with family photo shoot.

Paris was different than Atlanta or any place at home for that matter. You could go to a café and sit there for hours and hours on end without a sense of obligation or neediness. Sometimes a stranger would stop to say hello in attempt to make a new friend and that was fine too. Tajane walked the streets of Paris where her Mom and Dad had visited over twenty five years prior on their honey moon well before she came into being. She went with the tour guide and her bestie that Summer. The last Summer of their young adult lives.

The French air was warm and sweet. Bakeries and beautiful shoes by Roger Vivier, shopping, and fresh breakfast and salty buttery chocolate and butterscotch scents with a hint of honey suckle. Long stair cases, and classic street lamps in Montmartre. Boat rides through the city, and intricate architecture. There were giant cathedrals and fountains. It was beautiful and Tajane and Munier appreciated it and took plenty photos and made Instagram videos.

It was warm, people wore blue jeans, and shorts, and Parisian chic wear, colorful clothing and sunglasses.

There were red double decker buses just like London, and plenty of people in the streets and everywhere.

Florists of every kind. Music and bookstores everywhere. There were street performers and people selling things, street merchants, vintage clothing stores, and high end designer boutiques.

It was all there. The girls certainly weren't little children anymore. Men flirted with them relentlessly and they giggled about it.

Tajane was fluent but she never flexed around friends. She found it embarrassing and didn't feel like giving free lessons all day with people saying, "How do you say…" this and that of every variety.

So mostly she would listen and hear people talking about their kids, lovers, pets, food, Americans, embarrassing medical conditions, you name it.

She even overheard couple discussing the decision to take their kids to Disney Paris or church.

They decided on church and ice cream. There was always something to do in beautiful Paris, and not much of a dull moment.

The girls stayed in an Air B& B and everyone kept calling them sisters. There were trees everywhere. It was beautiful.

Tajane had the kind of loneliness you can only get while accompanied by a female when you prefer a male. The girls looked at each other…

"I know." They each said and laughed and went for cocktails.

Not of age in the states, there age seemed to be a non issue at the Parisian eateries and bars.

Some of the shops offered complimentary wine even.

They shopped at the Viaduct and took a ride over the Pont Neuf.

The last night in their Left Bank Air B&B they heard a squirrel in the ceiling above their room as they were near a small park. This made the last night there a scary adventure Tajane face timed her mom about.

Charity received her notification on her iphone.

"Mom we have something in our room!"

They were Felizfied and clinging to their perspective pillows on each side of the room.

"Where's Muneir baby?"

"I am here!" She chirped up in the background.

Charity and Sway payed for the trip and were accountable to Munier's mom if anything happened to her daughter while they were in France.

The flight the next morning was long, the two slept after they ate lunch at the airport.

The flight back to Atlanta was several hours and when they arrived a sign of relief came over them.

It was good to be headed home.

Tajane was still locked into a long conversation with the a young man who stole Munier's seat, and Munier thought surely she must have snagged his because she hadn't been interrupted in her sleep by any returning passenger to the empty seat she found.

There were a few more empty seats on the flight than expected, she realized as she looked around the cabin and noted four of the navy blue leather seats un occupied now since the short layover.

Munier wasn't sure how this man had captivated her always inquisitive but overly shy appearing friend Tajane. She was soft, her clothes always flowing somehow, her perfect beautiful smile was crisp and bright with her medium sized teeth perfectly aligned and her doe eyes reminiscent of her mother's. She was a curvy little thing, but not in access of her age, and she made nineteen look like the place to be.

Munier had no idea what the heck they were talking about but she noted the sudden silence.

The conversation had gone from passionate, mostly coming from him to her, something about black and white, and skyscrapers versus projects and Beyonce and Jay-Z to President Winfrey, and the fabric of America. Chicagoans versus New Yorkers and California versus Mexico for technology jobs, it was getting over Munier's head at about the fourth sentence.

She would hear her bestie's take on it all from a completely different, more fun, and simplified angle later anyway.

Now the fasten seat belt sign was on and the pair of them just four seats up across from Munier were a quiet duo. The young lady took notice of her friend, pausing for a moment and swung her head out of the isle nosily had he tried to kiss Tajane?

What the? They just met they were talking.

But no. He didn't.

Munier sighed a sign of relief for her friend.

He was looking at Tajane. His eyes were fiery and narrow yet fairly wide spread on his face.

Tajane looked back at him plainly. Was he trying to intimidate her?

Not a chance. Tajane was a box of words spilling out fragrantly into Shank's air space dazzling him until all he could do was force a pause.

She had met him on every subject. Unbelievable.

Shank was the type of dude who really believed deep down that women might be smarter than men but acted is if men were smarter than women.

Tajane's breath smelled like spearmint gum.

They had started talking sex, astrology, and religion now.

Now Shank looked deep into her eyes. She was kind. She hadn't told him this seat was taken, though he figured it out when the other young lady approached from the bathroom and reluctantly sat behind them.

"Come with me." He announced dryly to Tajane, ever curious as to what she would do next.

The fasten seatbelts sign flicked on and he unbuckled his and jumped up so quick.

'Where could they possibly be going, on a plane?'

Taj reluctantly unfastened her seatbelt and got up.

"Sir!" a flight attendant called clearly from the front of the International flight to the back of the plane where Shank darted into the restroom as if on cue.

Taj followed him ducking low as if it would make her invisible somehow.

He reached out just as he squeezed into the bathroom compartment and pulled her in with him.

The airline stewardess gawked and rolled her eyes a moment.

"Kayla, I swear girl. Every damn Parisian flight."

"What?" asked the woman's coworker.

"Somebody boning in the bathroom girl."

"They better sit they butt down before they get tossed. The pilot is landing the plane!"

Shank latched the door behind Tajane. She wore a silky sundress. She leaned back on the tiny wall space facing the toilet and her grabbed her waist and pulled her into him as if he would be un affected by her in every way but too late, he was already intoxicated, mesmerized by the mingling of their young minds.

Tajane let out a breath and Shank made a motion to kiss her. Their mouth's were close…he turned her whole body towards the door of the airplane's compact restroom, sliding her passed the small manual sink to the back of the door.

With his right hand he traced her silhouette with the back of his middle and index finger.

With his left hand he unlatched the door, and the two of them nearly toppled out but Tajane kept her footing in her grass bottom wedges.

Shank had breathed on her neck warmly and boldly as he reached for the door handle and the two of them were suddenly in the aisle walking back to the seats the leapt out of only moments before.

The plane's chimes rang, 'Ting, ting, ting'

"Would ALL passengers please return to their seats as the fasten seatbelt sign is active and we are approaching our landing at the Hartsfield Atlanta airport." The flight attendant tried to sound pleasant and calm as her job demanded but was truly admittedly bothered at the obvious lack of respect from these two young travelers.

"Fasten your seatbelt girl." Shank said to Tajane as he let her out of his romantic clutches back into the airplanes center aisle.

They were out of breath and plopped down into their seats and he held her hand.

He was gonna get the girl, and she was simply taken with him and that is how it was from day one.

Tajane's heart beat so fast and the two of them clicked their seatbelt latches in place while both were amused at their light weight outlawdedness.

Had that just happened? He hadn't kissed her.

He had barely even touched her yet there seemed to be this statement.

There seemed to be this declaration and she could feel it start. It was made of something she could feel, but not see, sense, but not taste or smell. It was made of time, reasons and possibilities and it wove firmly yet comfortably around them both and that is where it started.

Munier inched up to the isle beside the newly forming couple.

"Sooooo….are you guys ready?"

Tajane realized her friend had the same impression the flight attendants must have had earlier. But being the spunky young lady she was she merely played along.

"I don't know…the flight was pretty intense." She said in her best exaggerated sexy voice.

Munier rolled her eyes and Shank held his composure.

He wanted the approval of everyone who knew his new lady love and this one must be pretty important if they flew to Paris together and she didn't even put up a fuss about him taking her seat on the plane. She was pretty too, and had bestie written all over her.

"So…who is your new friend?"

Taj blushed. She didn't even know this man's government name.

"Shank." He said dryly. "Shank Cole."

"Munier Mansala" Tajane's best friend murmured. He was a fine ass white boy, mixed boy whatever.

Everybody seemed to pause for a minute.

Was his name really…Shank? He seemed a little rough around the edges but not so much to have a thug name like that.

Taj looked at Munier and shrugged. She knew her friend would prod and scold her later with the best imitation of a concerned parent she could muster. They wouldn't make it to the airport ladies room without something being said.

Tajane could bet on it.

Taj and Shank exchanged info and gave a long lingering hug in which he sexily and almost startlingly whispered in her ear, "I like you Miss."

She shook her head in agreement, "Mm hm" and he let go gently and they said goodbye.

"Okay, now I know you KNOW we gotta talk!"

Munier started.

She spoke this enthusiastically as soon as Shank boarded his train from D gate and headed to transport.

He seemed to know it was time to make an eager exit rather than linger in the wake of Taj's best friend and her awkward ogling.

"Okay Taj!" She simply declared. "Are you serious right now!?"

Taj shrugged.

"Oh ok. The cat's really got your tongue.

Did you…nah. I know you didn't just joint the mile high club just now…"

Munier went on both playfully and eagerly.

Her soft brown eyes were big and dark. She was as curious as could possibly be at her friend's new found fortune in romance.

Taj finally spoke, "Like what does that even mean? Do you know?!" she laughed.

Then she bowed her friend lightly nudging her and pulled her to her side.

"Moonie! You KNOW. I just met him.

He is fine and all but he ain't bout to get my v card on an airplane for real."

Munier sighed a big sigh of relief.

Then Taj did a dab, "She's still intact that's a fact!" She said loudly.

"Munier was super relieved, "GOOD, because girl your Daddy AND your Mama would kill us BOTH on some Scandal, How to Get Away With Murder type ish!"

Then Tajane was quiet up until they got their luggage, and she was still sheepishly looking around for her new found boy friend.

She had never met anyone like Shank he was cool, soulful, and fresh like laundry, but his energy dark and mysterious like night time in a strange new place.

He was swift, fast and witty, he seemed to have come from nowhere, and slipped back into nowhere.

Tajane finally spoke…"Ok so he was like 'come here', and then I thought he was going to kiss me, and he didn't and then we were back in our seats. That fast, like super-fast.

"Oooooh." Munier said. "He sounds slick. Is he a player? He might be a player girl, watch out for that one."

"THANK YOU seed of doubt." Tajane rolled her eyes, they got their bags and caught the Uber home to the McDaniel's family home.

It had been a long, busy productive week.

Work, bills, errands, church, non profit, neighborhood meeting, date night had been moved to a middly of the week lunch with her husband which Charity was fine with because they got their freak on in the car and that was fun, they hadn't even done that since before their one and only daughter was born let alone a baby.

Sway satisfied Charity now the way he had before they had even ever made love for the very first time at all that time at his grandmother's house, their first home.

She counted herself a lucky woman at the least.

He was a good father, and though things sparkled less at times due to the natural withering of time, he always took strides for his family to feel special and know they were first.

Sway was not the kind of man who did things for other's attention, but more the type of man who moved operating on purpose.

He was always considering the other guy which Charity found one of his most noble characteristics.

Her husband was stronger now and he kept fitness a priority in his life. Sometimes she would marvel at where he found the time.

She did the same so it wasn't impossible but his extraordinary ability to stay in a league of his own, limitless, dreaming up new business ventures and big money making schemes that saved the youth, and women who suffered from domestic violence, and homeless Americans is what wielded his wife and his community's respect.

Charity loved. He would share these details of pragmatic day to day business and elevating ventures that would take a small town proprietor to commercial main stream in a 2 year time frame, and at the end he would say, and 'this will help save the world by 'blank' and he would insert cause.

She laughed in pride and joy from her mouth to God's ears at her husband's goodness and clever ways.

The two of them never had time to do basic things like watch television, but their music game was strong.

Charity loved the new rappers, and singers of today because they would always do a free show or two for any one of their benefit events at the drop of a dime.

Sway loved this about her, she had an impeccable and uncanny ability to transform any and everything he gave her from money, time, attention, even a compliment and transform it into pure gold. Charity wasn't about just keeping her man, Charity was about keeping her family and everyone in her life happy. She learned how to give people what they needed and would go until it was time for her to relax and replenish. She did that at church every Sunday and this made a balanced life for her. She was one of the very few members of the church who could check a ministry if they got too grabby with the people's time. Charity was swift to grow the church and put a new member to work.

She kept more South West Atlanta youth off the street than the Boy's and girls club of America and everyone conscious and aware of the human cause in the community could see that.

People respected the McDaniel's family and I suppose they had earned it over time. Not many could say they withstood the economic changes they had, and that gave people a sense of hope and inspiration.

Sway had launched his Money Chaser program on V103 and had the support of well known Atlanta Dj Frankski and Wanda's Morning show and many others.

Atlanta had become a radio mecca and offers were pouring in.

Sway kept his celebrity image clean, he was loyal to his wife, always spoke of keeping God first and family next after that.

He had his share of female followers. One of which was Ms. Feliz Bilsom, a media queen from NYC who had made her escape from the Bronx, NY to Atlanta just four years prior.

She worked as a Publicist Assistant for Future, Drake, Rick Ross, Monami Entertainment and formulated Love and Hip Hop with the impeccable and legendary Mona Scott Young, Yandy Smith Harris, a slew of the best looking Atlanta attorneys were her friends, and the folks at CNN,and even local news stations. People knew her face and they knew her name. Corin Fox had recently cited her in a Good Morning America Interview for helping promote her new film, and even Mike Burnett, Tyrese, Dwayne the Rock Johnson, and Kevin Hart, Ron Howard, and

Steven Spielburg who slayed the television programming and now film game for decades.

Ms. Feliz was sensuous, and if Sway could see her, really look into her soul, he would never be able to deny her his love, nor would any other man for that matter.

She was a widow. Word on the street was her husband was a leading Neurologist at Emory and had a heart attack and died.

It was rumoured that he had an amphetamine addiction and that is what led to his demise.

He had a nick name in the Hip hop community, as 'Jitt ' short for legit, and short for the jitters.

He was a fun loving, pleasant man, not with all of the pomp and circumstance many Atlanta professionals hid behind.

Jitt was fun loving, and playful. He rubbed shoulders with the best but he would say, "Dr. Jitt! Don't forget!" and people would always laugh, at that same stale one liner joke because it was him all day.

Ms. Bilsom went silent after he died, but she inherited a substantial 8 million dollar award from his life insurance policy, and could do with that what she pleased.

Most of which went into her television series productions, and a new reality show she spawned called 'Factory Wars.'

She dated Will.i.Am for a while, and the two were rumoured to have conceived a son, but rumours were just that and the both of them had hush money enough that the story swiftly dissipated almost as soon as it mysteriously emerged.

Mrs. Bilsom liked white men, and she had these jade green eyes that they loved as well.

Nas car curves dizzied even the most self absorbed male preffering of men, and most recently Usher introduced her to yet another Mr.

Legendary of the moment.

Usher was always trying to hook people up. Him and Music Soulchild…they wanted everybody to be happy in love together.

Pharrell was also but he would hand his people a NDA and constitute and produce the entire relationship down to the color of sox they wore in public. Of course his relationships always started out as media fabric, but sometimes they turned real.

Mr. Williams was gifted in that the people he introduced, quite often stayed together for life.

His family nick name behind was Preacher, for that reason.

Ms. Feliz sexed them all. The name of her game after her husband died was 'Bed that.'

She made a point of having drinks with the most high profile names in business, music entertainment, and the medical field to satisfy her lonely overblown ego.

But Sway…she could not.

Feliz followed him around in her head. She peaked at his comings and goings until she began to be where he was and he still hadn't taken notice. It had been over a year and her obsession didn't fade. Her thoughts of him only grew stronger. She stared at his image in magazine articles, and built a vision board in her mind which Sway was the center of.

Sure, Feliz knew he was married, in fact to her, so was she.

The best part of her heart had died along with her late husband, Dr.Jitt.

Eli was his actual name.

She loved poetry. It was a quiet passion and the most sane part of this baroness millionaire with the quiet eyes and a bad booty. Every man wanted her, but what she wanted she couldn't have unless…

She loved an author's poem called Leaves from a poetry book she wrote called Sativa Strains.

Leaves

Leafs from fallen leaves

Autumn is what you are, rain from fallen rain, it's clear you are a star. Jade of jaded love, no lover could compare, to your light, to your night, to your water, to your air.

Some late nights alone in her Paces Ferry Condo

Mrs. Bilsom would read these poems and cry in her Moscato, thinking about a man like Sway.

Her attraction was severe, but private.

She made his hands hers and made love to herself fantasizing about his breath next to her neck and it worked every time.

Charity knew her man was wanted by any hot blooded female in town with half a brain, many men even lusted after her husband although he was straight. She also trusted her husband to life, and would no more believe this country boy to cheat than a purple unicorn come to life.

Nothing stood between her and the love, respect, honor, and trust she had for her husband Swaynick Mcdaniels.

The McDaniel's family was as strong as her husband's name and no man could even hold a match to him. Atlanta was full of handsome, wealthy, prominent men of color, gay straight, Latino, Asian, White, all types, shapes, sizes and ages most attached in one way or another, but all of that could change in the blink of an eye come Summertime, or a lonely Winter.

Charity was no fool. But every growing pain she experienced drew she and her husband closer.

She stood across the kitchen island just behind her gorgeous daughter. These moments were rare and ever fleeting.

She quietly kissed her on the forehead, startling her a tiny bit.

"Oh." She jumped-"I thought you were Dad…"

"Oh shoot, did I disappoint you dear?"

The evidence that Taj was her parents only daughter was ever present and evident in her mother's tone. Charity was a verbally affectionate and warm mother who would do anything for Tajane and this was not unappreciated by either of them. Yet there was a secret now.

Tajane knew telling her mother of her new found beau would be exactly the same as telling her father, and she dared not. Shank was mysterious and foreign to her family environment. She ached to share this part of her life with him, but knew it could spell disaster for their love and life together.

He was too hood for her father and Taj truly believed he would forbid her to see him if he knew his baby girl had her first real boyfriend who was on probation for being an accessory to armed robbery before he was twenty five years old, no matter how much he worked hard on the daily to prove he left that life behind including cutting himself off from any and everyone he knew during the time, and….well, Shank was it.

Tajane was only turning twenty years old…and the connection she had with Shank seemed already to form an awkward space between Tajane and her mother all though she was certain her dad was oblivious still and that gave her a peace.

Munier was right, they were in the digital age and a person could live multiple lives if they so desired and no one may ever find out, but at the same time nothing was sacred and all was revealed through the internet. They suffered the 'Millenial plight' in this way.

It was there in front of Charity at at the Breast cancer awareness, 'Think Pink' fundraiser.

Fabulous art was on display at the High…

Great Atlanta artists, like the prolific Jeff Ewing, Justin Bua, Kolongi Braithwaite, Gordon Parks Flash photography exhibit, Shahida, the colorful geometry of Maurice Evans.

Kahinde Wiley's fantastic depiction of president Barak Obama and black Jesus, saints and families in stain glassed greatness, The fabulous textures of Jamea Richmond-

Edwards,Fabric, sculpture, rich paintings come to life peeling gracefully out of the backdrop.

And Henry Battle with his classic black romance depictions... Nathaniel Mary Quinn and his keileidescopic healing rituals on open canvas, frameless, limitless art. But among all of these great works of art from great Black American Artists...

There was a disturbing portrait emerging.

A woman in a yellow dress with a neckline than plunged down to her navel stood gazing at her husband from across the room. Her stance said words Charity herself was mesmerized at this woman's movement.

Who was she?

She stared at Sway as if he were the evening's entertainment. Her gaze sizzled and compelled Sway's attention.

He was standing next to two of his colleagues Dj Nabs, L.L. Cool J, Tyler Perry, 50 Cent, Magic Johnson, Busta Rhymes, and Shaquille O'neal were there.

His boys looked across so player at what he was looking at but they saw lust in a tangible ribbon electrifying the room from in front of a Marcus Williams with Frank Morrison boldness.

She was the sun in that damn dress, and she was about to give Sway sunburn.

Charity could not move. She saw pure power exuding from this female across the room to her husband Sway whom the woman in the yellow dress gazed at like a big fat snack as though she were a starving lioness ready to pounce.

Charity would relish the stranger's admirations of what was hers usually but this gave her pause.

Sway looked little, helpless, and antagonized and this bothered Charity. His usual King confidence sparkle had melted into a trickle of nearly smellable masculine vulnerability.

Charity was uncomfortable seeing her husband in this woman's odd light, and this was a never before occurance.

Charity took a deep breath and became the better part of Sway allowing the tractor beam of energy to instead magnetize her own physical form. She approached autonomously yet focused and determined to break the flow of this woman's attention on what was and always would be painfully out of Feliz's reach.

"Now that is an f um girl dress, right *there!*"

Charity McDaniels was hilarious under fire, and just regular comedic on any given day anyway.

She had charm and had learned to make people laugh as her super power. She could use her sexual confidence and energy to connect with whomever posed as potential opposition and have them eating from her hand's palm with glee.

Those who couldn't respect her purpose, were left flailing on the wayside of social situations to replay their own pain at the lack of humorous essence they possessed and could only piece together later that Charity was loving them and teaching them to live at the same time through her graceful witt and attention.

Mission accomplished.

Charity would not stoop, but disrespect was never tolerated. She would make herself known.

Feliz was so caught off guard that for a moment she felt silly for wearing something so over the top sexy to appeal to any onlookers or victims as they were well thought of persons generally and the woman who came into the midst of the line of direction Sway and his colleague were in, made Sway look like a dusty dude, even as well as he was dressed and a brotha to the side if one hadn't known any better.

"Girl you must have borrowed that one from Ms.
Kim without Ms. Manaj finding out about it, that dress is speechless on you."

Charity whipped her honey tongue all over this big yellow ray of sexual sunshine headed for her husband's life and she evaporated.

Feliz looked from across the room into Sway's eyes. The three and a half dates he had taken her on of pure ecstasy twenty years before flooded both their memories and she blushed with every evidence that he was now happily married.

Feliz was a sex bomb. She had tattoos on her curvaceous thighs and a slit in that yellow organza dress that heated all of Summer.

She spun around and it flared ever so slightly on the green as the live band played that Friday night at The High.

"What a scene,…" She murmured under her breath.

"Oh shit. Man you see that?" 50 tapped Sway's arm and he hung his head down quickly to the floor.

Sway remembered how he had traded Reesha for Feliz, and shoved her far to the back of his mind when he realized he had two potential stalkers on his hands rather than one.

Feliz was not hood like Reesha, but rather a classier chic who appeared at least to have come from a decent family and all but Charity came after Reesha and that was that.

He didn't see her anymore after going off on a business trip before he opened the first office of his firm. He felt she didn't need him, that she was too beautiful for him and would fare better without him and said as much to her.

He had devastated this twenty four year old aspiring actress and model, and it was a heartbreak she desperately tried to let go of but could not.

'What was she doing here?' Her full breasts were richly flattered by the ruffle on her dress, and there was a slit in it's skirt that screamed high end fashion, and revenge.

She was thick and curvaceous but it was clear that she had cared for herself.

Sway had been tempted plenty before, Atlanta was chalk full of beautiful, powerful women of color. Amazonian types, exotic looking mixed girls, and a range of beautiful people. Ambitious ones, talented and hungry ones chasing fame, the American dream, or just true love.

Sway made it his business to know who they all were.

His clients were pro athletes, entrepreneurs, small mom and pop businesses, veterinarians, to dentists mostly people of color one way or another but he also worked with white restaurant owners, golf club owners, film studios, and Atlanta Braves and plenty of Atlanta's high cotton.

Sway's lower region came to mild attention on medium as he realized the beauty of this woman was emanating beyond the space between himself and his wife he had never experienced anything like it all of the memories of the times I'll be at brief that he spent earlier in his life with this woman surged through him as he remembered the Times They chilled, laughed drank, were merry, smoked, danced, enjoyed the music together, kissed in stair wells, holding hands in the street, sexed in bathtubs, had tickle fights that ended in passionate love making, enjoying one another's touch smile and skin and he vaguely remembered himself pondering if she could be his soulmate. Feliz's beauty was prominent and it emulated everything he ever wanted to stand for and represent in his life and his community. To look at her she was a pillar and an obvious queen

"Bruh I got to know about this I got to know what the f*** just went on I never even seen you make that face before you are looking so cray right now your shoes like that damn interesting Brougham what the f*** wuh goin on who who that who is that chick that's what I want to know."

Sway›s long time partner Cassius Greenberg stood next to him all kinds of gobsmacked.

"The booty on her alone, got am."

The mood shifted in the gallery space as the live band's drummer was suddenly f****** it up acting as if he had a whole fight with the atmosphere with in the museum walls and heads turned it was the infamous Lil John Roberts smashing along side Big bucket and the infamous Spanky Mcurdy and Ken Ford displayed his electrifying violin skills throughout the evening with Bonita Jalane, Algebra Blesset and Chloe x Halle harmonizing right along.

Each briefly in town and obviously auditioning for the new Tyler Perry movie, which was this abstract documentary about race in America reported to be the most serious film

Black Entertainment had ever seen today's date. It was to be titled, "Dear Black People," and would be the most controversial, potent, truth telling, forward facing and multi faceted real life point of view of real white Americans and their actual real life experiences and views on people of color in America ever documented.

The script had only been released to two major filmmakers in the US and one overseas everyone in and around the entertainment industry was buzzing with curiosity about this phenomenal new project and thrilled at the variety the ever prolific creative genius Tyler Perry would be working along side his long time mentor Spike Lee. studios and its coherts consistently making the city of Atlanta an oozing and buzzing thoroughly inspiring and productive major media capital. Beauty and talent were everywhere and the city with a gentle but loud hum.

It buzzed loud and there was so much money to be made in the city pursuing one's dreams as all creatives were new found friends and a new kind of harmony was present in the production rooms, and cutting room floors; equality was on the rise and love in the air.

Sway couldn't talk he left the space he was standing in and walked over to Tiny and TI's trap Museum Blues exhibit.

The piece featured some of the best pieces from their trap Museum and a very rare hip hop piece for the culture that demonstrated the conflict between different genres in Black American music versus love, war, struggle, dominance, from gang violence, drug abuse, and domestic violence.

The mixed media art work have been featured in Forbes Magazine Black Enterprise and was touring and also on display at the Hip Hop Museum in Bronx New York. It would finish up in the Smithsonian with a one and only 5x5 print being featured in American Music Hall of Fame.

Sway's head spun. It just seemed completely unfair in that moment everything he thought life was had a slant on it it was like he smoked a big fat blunt and it was stronger and more wild then any high he had ever expected even though his days of partake it ended in high school.

"I need a drink matter fact I need a whole bottle."

His wife nearly disappeared. Feliz became the most beautiful woman in the room. The guilt stung, only wildly overshadowed by an invisible energetic type of warrants that could only be described as lust with deep yearning.

Sway watched as men walked up to her trying to get her attention to no avail deep down he knew she was there for him. Where she had come from with a mystery where she would return to the same.

Sway watch that's his beautiful light- skinned long haired wife emerged between himself and this mystery woman in the yellow dress she seemed to exchange some light words that you laughed and Feliz spun around walking toward the other side of the room.

Something peculiar in sway sunk as he came to the vague realization that this woman from his past may have been clearly unaware that he was attached and he had no idea that she had any feeling or wearing a 7 whatsoever anymore but in that moment Clarity seem to merge into the light for for three adults.

Perhaps it wasn't clear but something was certainly felt.

Feliz spun around the butterflies within her flap their wings ferociously but she remembered the effect of Sway's energy on her life force she was aware that she was at her most vulnerable with him and that given the opportunity he could have her easily even elegantly without protest. Tears threatened to well up in her eyes and she just yourself harshly for the patheticness of her desires.

She was determined to keep smiling and so she did but gently walk towards Corridor in the back of the room that lead to the women's Lounge so she could collect herself.

Sway turned around Charity was talking to their daughter laughing with Tajane and Muniere's parents now.

Kayla, the gorgeous mother of Tajane's dearest friend locked her eyes with Charity's.

"I saw the whole thing. I saw the whole thing girl" Grinning, and kee kee-ing.

The two women laughed and had become sort of a catchphrase between the two of them and a private joke something special and sacred between friends acknowledging the plight of each has wifehood.

It was a similar and complementary acknowledgement the two of them knew Which meant very simply that they supported each other and keeping a key principle of marriage seeing and not seeing hearing and not hearing knowing and not knowing Feliz wouldn't cry at least not yet the loneliness she had been experiencing after breaking up with Marcus during the pandemic had become so unbearable she spent hours in yoga taking walks alone going to movies alone fantasizing in the shower doing the best you could to Manifest this love with sway home she had come to the harsh and painful realization was not available and for Exquisite reason. His wife was beautiful and her energy was magnanimous.

Charity appeared to Feliz to be the type of woman that could easily have any man she wanted regardless of his position in life and though she resented competing with other women or women who competed with other women she knew she was no match 4 Sway's wife despite her quakening inner notion that she was his true soulmate.

Marcus called her phone just then. Dad never been the type of couple with many romantic nuances not traditional in any kind of way having met at work very practical and conveniently arranged in each other's life buy a very common event gradually growing into friendship and then actually having a conversation and deciding that perhaps they could try pair up which eventually fostered a type of romantic interest and attraction between the two of them.

It was a very practical arrangement. Like basically like the same je ne sais quoi that she had experience in relationships prior especially the one with sway.

Sway felt divine he felt universally ordered to be her lover and her body responded to this truth. Marcus was younger than her and his touch was awkward cold and some ways static, well intended but somewhat sterile, not fluid in fiery like what she'd experienced with a few lovers past. And certainly not the magical heat of sways touch.

She danced privately with the best discretion she could to the rhythmic cadence her memories of Swaynick McDaniel's gave in her darkest hours.

It was as though she was a Sculptor and he was her Muse and her thoughts of him thing to shape his life as she was ever careful to remain thinking highly of him for his best outcome. Feliz got high off of this love and Feliz used this love to numb her pain and give her reasons to live. She was divorced, widowed, childless and now somewhere between Sex and the City and Being Mary Jane.

But in her heart and her mind he was the one for whom she would risk it all gladly.

"have you seen my green sweatshirt?"

His text was typical Marcus. They had dated off and on for nearly three years, and finally moved in together against each of their better judgement.

He had finally learned how to have better sex with her, all though it was sometimes once a month and he had learned to stop leaving his clothes lying around, but still drank more than she was comfortable with, also he lied like a little boy, and she had caught him picking the crust out of his eyes and eating it.

Then there were the Instagram models, sex workers, video games, and could be cheap as hell, all of which both frightened and disgusted the stunningly beautiful though, highly sought after and vuluptousFeliz.

His awkward and seemingly trivial q & a was a go to to check on her many times and she did all she could to remain respectful to him because he had believed in her Publicist business when no one else did and she was grateful. Still these were often things he already knew the answers to or that she could have no idea on.

Harry walked into the women's lounge with her feet making the ever soft clicking sound her Max Azria heels lended to the marble flooring beneath her feet. The evening had grown later and she was relieved to find that she was the only person in the ladies room at that moment. The museum passed on hiring concierge service for the event to the dismay of its organizers but the high ceilings and bright glow of excellent lighting surrounding four foot beveled mirrors and live background music sufficed the evenings ambiance.

Feliz's eyes grew wet she looked down at herself all dressed up in this bright yellow dress flirting with taking the room and nearly damned herself.

Looking deeply into her own eyes she flashed back to the times she spent with Sway McDaniels ever so jaded in her memory. He was her light.

Every time when she was squeezed in the tight, stifling, and soul squishing confinement of a mental emotional jail cell trapped in the throes of an abusive marriage through time and space she remembered his smile.

When all hope was gone and she had nowhere to live no money no options for sustaining herself other than to sell her body she remembered his smile.

When Dorado passed…

The darkness of Life the pain the strife is struggling to hurt the oppression the racial tensions and discrimination she faced summer times in the Georgia heat taking any job she could to survive and care for herself with menial ends sacrificing her own femininity morals values ethics safety trying her best to prove that she could survive her early beginnings. Feliz was a twin. A caseworker at her local DFCS have been overheard speaking 2 a child advocate about her and her sister being found in a garbage dump and raised by a local clergyman and his wife.

She struggled and carried with her this deep sense of loss feeling so large as if it would engulf her like a canyon deep and hurt the middle of her full of Despair grief and rejection and every day she struggled with this thing trying to doll herself up and show up, find new clients and provide the best possible service to existing ones, she struggled to hold her chin high find reasons to live she had no children. Her former relationship left her barren and she often likened herself the Jesus is woman at the well.

Feliz ached to keep a sense of pride and strength about her self dignity hoping and praying every day some days for the will to live.

Many nights she cried asking God why.

Why was she born why was she here?

Why did she need to be on this Earth if the very ones who were blessed with her presence threw her away.

Trusting people was out of the question.

Feliz had been raped twice by the time she was 4 years old. In her preteens and teens she never dated boys they merely challenged her to casual meaningless and devaluing sex not respecting her or treasuring her. There were no kind words even in flattery. General courtship was rather replaced with harshness, slander disrespect, physical and emotional pulling, pushing, being slapped in the face, she was worthless and she often struggled with guilt for not giving in and her fellow students slandering her hating her calling her names making up rumors which had nothing to do with her character, saying she was places with people that she didn't even associate with. She had been in and out of foster care living among strangers, Ministers, do-gooders, pervert manipulators and narcissist those who presented themselves in the best light but we're no better than others except for the willingness to take a risk to be of "help" in the life of a wayward child like her. They got paid. Some had children of their own. Some could not deal with her long term and decided she was not ' a good fit.'

There would be shiny black Hefty bags that seem to follow her everywhere she went like Mary's Little lamb and she would be one place for two weeks another place for three months, another place for 4 days, another place overnight, maybe there a weekend, she would have to sleep on a pull out bed in or trundle in the middle of the floor. Or a sleeping bag on a wiry old coiled matress, bunk beds, and there would be, three other girls in the room with her with no space for her to even turn around she was State Property, born a ward of the court, often her Foster brothers, and sometimes sisters taking a liking to her after she had built some means of trust, later waking to gum in her hair, roaches in her pillow case, their hands upon her or within her in the night...she had years of therapy which mostly consisted of paid professional strangers listening to her with bleak glances from halfway across the room.

Some would cry.

She tried to commit suicide at 7 years old.

Her weak cold flaccid young body found on one of her foster parents sofa after school by a friend's parent when dropping Anaya Sutterfield off for a playdate.

Mrs. Sutterfield called 911 and an ambulance came to rush to the E.R. and pump the seven year old Feliz's stomach of its contents as she had overdosed on something she found in the cabinet and a bottle of wine. She just wanted the pain to stop, to go to sleep, have happy dreams, and not have to worry about it starting all over again, the neglect and absence of her drug addicted, alcoholic mentally ill parents waking up.

The little girl could not pronounce the name of the medication but the label said on the bottle:

May cause drowsiness
Alcohol may make this worse
Use care when operating a vehicle vessel or dangerous machinery.

Her own seven-year-old life was the dangerous machinery and the pain she felt began to manifest physically in her body. Feliz would ache and her bones always a sense of guilt for something that she couldn't see, ostracized for being in the system or at times not knowing what it was and always this aching many times it would keep her up at night she would wake with dark circles under her eyes children at school with take turns calling her raccoon girls further bruising herself image and esteem.

This was Feliz's whole story though she had planted a fabulous one in it's place.

Her childhood a myriad of deeply scaring emotional abuse and rejection, commonplace neglect and different and those stupid shiny black Hefty bags that served as some type of luggage they always stretched they always got holes in them and Feliz learned how to wear only what she could wash in a single load of laundry and only keep seven days worth of clothing at any given time.

And her adult life she began to read self-improvement books attending church moving through various schools of thought and sometimes cults and shrouded business opportunities, seeking answers and the face of God for relief. These things had promises of Salvation, Grace and get rich quickness.

The sky pie.

It was at one of these events that she met Dorado Octavius Newsome or "Don."

He was an attractive enough black man with Island features face-full skin dark as deep chocolate so much so that his friends and family refer to him as 'The chocolate Don'

He seemed to be magnetized by something within Feliz and drawn to her like bees to honey walking evenly across the room to engage asking her for her phone number or any way he could get to know her better. His energy was intense his presence was big and hungry toward her it was unlike anything she'd ever experienced from another human being in her life he wanted her and it was plane. Dorado would stop at nothing to get her.

Feliz recalled being at a family Barbecue with him he has some cousins from different stock down in Florida, unlike him and his sister both of whom were educated by a single mother with trades and specialties. They came from the projects and were the mouthy type.

Dorado's cousin Glenn glanced at Feliz upon first meeting the couple.

They had only known each other for a month at the time.

"Nigga bring your old Doritos stinking ass over here, Dorado Octavius Newsome!"

"Gimme a hug boy gimmee a hug! I love you man. I love this man right here y'all!"

He said amusingly to his other relatives, as they crowded around the swimming pool area.

A tall light-skinned freckled cousin of his grabbed him and embraced him in a bro hug, the two of them laughing and cackling like teenage boys. Don's mother's sister's children from Panama City. They were real hood. They had both their mama and daddy but their daddy had a side chick across town with four other children and word on the street was that the lady was their mothers best friend, a chic named Lonnie.

Don hadn't even met his other cousins only hearing of them as proverbial black sheep and distant relatives, while his Aunt Judy kept Swift her only child and baby boy.

The man hugging Feliz's brand new self-imposed boyfriends name was Swift.

He played basketball and had recently gotten drafted into the pro leagues as a bench men for the Miami Heat which meant a trail of women from all over the world followed him around on social media and sometimes in actual life and he could never just pick one.

"Ayyye cuzzo! You ever marry Sheila?"

Don hit Swift's soft-spot head on and Straightaway.

Swift hated being the only achiever on his side of the family but the one thing he hated more than that was not having anyone to share it with.

"Nah. Who is this!?"

Swift said playfully and partially licking his lips as he looked at his cousin's brand new girlfriend's face.

"How do you plan on keeping her playa? She know you fix cars right?"

He cajoled and joned his cousin while his eyes shined and he boldly admired Feliz closely inching toward a rabbit hair from disrespect.

Swift was a very serious dude.

Ambitious and bold rarely a gentleman he liked to believe he could set his eyes on something and get it regardless of what it was and now that included Feliz.

"Hi my name is Swift. He›s a clown. My cousin is a clown.

Don't say I didn't warn you."

He gave her a side hug.

"Good luck. What›s your name?"

"Feliz."

"Damn you pretty. Okay so good luck."

Everybody turned around and moved toward the kitchen to get plates and eat.

There was fresh macaroni and cheese, BBQ Beef Ribs, fried catfish with mustard, collard greens, pork chops, German chocolate cake, peach cobbler, apple cobbler, Aunt Tuesday's 7-Up cake, orange Crush Soda, grape Crush Soda, baked ham, two pans of Jiffy cornbread, some fresh tamales from the tamale lady, tacos & fresh rolled chicken flautas, guacamole, salsa, sour cream, from Marialana; Don's cousin Chuchee's wife, and Zack brought daiquiris because he and his boyfriend were in from Lafayette. Everyone was laughing there were a few kids in the family at that time and the group played dominoes and Spades in small clusters.

They had gathered that first Fourth of July in the fashion of a family reunion at Atlanta Doctors Taft & Jenny Newsome's house in East Cobb not far from the future home of Sway and Charity unbeknownst to Feliz with Sway having then become a recent memory to her freshly broken heart has he ghosted her just months before post having a brief argument about the status of their newly forming relationship and he faded away into his rapidly evolving career and entreprenueralship only to be seen again on magazine covers, t.v. and radio. Feliz bowed her head, she was ashamed, she had chased him, phone stalkingly, missing him, awkward and trying to know what to say, believing she loved him and she carried on for years until he finally changed his number.

He told her bluntly she needed help and it was only then that she could see how sick she truly had become, obsessed with the hope that he would one day love her in return, unable to see her own personal power or beauty, casting all discretion aside, so egoless chasing, wasting, precious time, energy, and resource, as she faded away from her own personal identity into a false version of herself, and then one day she stopped. He had changed his number and she hers and each went on in opposite directions just like that, She saw a doctor, he prescribed her a good anti-depressant, and she started up therapy and let go of the chasing behavior for twenty years, everything changed, all but the love she knew she had deeply, discreetly tucked away for his smile, his touch, his sensual essence. She made him her fantasy and dream lover and in this way he became so much better in illusion than he ever could have been in life for Feliz. This time would be different.

She had seen his billboards, heard of various speaking engagements but opted not to go so as not to be sucked into phone stalking behaviors and unrequited love shit again. Then the pandemic came about and Marcus became periodically dismissive, and in the worst of ways, entertaining other women, comparing her to television celebrities and pop stars, he broke up with her in the middle of the pandemic, and her soul crumbled so sure that although he was imperfect and even a little gross at times, he *loved* her. It wasn't until he broke up with her for a third time that she realized that perhaps she had simply gone wrong so many years ago. She was younger, in her twenties then. She pondered and pontificated to her ownself trying to determine any or all possible outcomes of her running into Swaynick,

She grabbed her journal, went to bible studies, the gym, fasted, did all she could do to break free from this self inflicted love spell that only Sway seemed to be the benefactor of. Oddly Feliz was satisfied just knowing he was alive and well, somewhere, as she knew he was certainly a catch any woman could love. It perplexed her and she continued to shove it out of her mind, but tonight, she was here.

Feliz dried her hands and left the bathroom, and he was there.

It was Sway, standing directly infront of her in the dimmed lighting of the restroom corridor. Time stopped, there was only the breath of another, It was as if they had this secret telepathic and unspoken agreement and vow to their attraction, The two embraced. They were nearly alone, The powerfully engulfing stillness of the present moment surrounded them as their magnets fit hand in glove, and lock in key.

Feliz knew he was there. She took a risk, but if the world was coming to an end as it clearly was, she could not bare to allow her ego to keep her away. She wanted to look into his eyes again. If she got Covid, she could die happy knowing she had one more moment with him no matter what.

Feliz was swallowed whole in his warm embrace. The heat from his body seeping into hers through his Tom Ford suit.

The butterflies danced and quivered. There was the essence of taboo justified by the simple nuance that love justifies all things, and although those were not the words spoken, the mage cog their union was as real to her as her own breath, Besides, it was prudent for her business to be there and they both knew it.

Sway had only ever wanted the very best for Feliz. He knew she was a wounded soul, and she must have suffered from his absence despite the annoyance and distaste he felt from her persuing him. They had become so lopsided in their energy, there were times he was paranoid and not wanting to go out thinking any lover of hers would jealously find him and try to tarnish his reputation or worse commit assault. She was a beautiful woman. Many men wanted her and it was evident, but she just could not see herself and so she chased him rather than accepting that he was moving on right where he was, and he continually convinced himself it was the right thing, without realizing what she was doing she buried her lips into his neck feeling his strong. Long, hard electrifying member. He could rule the world with his erection in that moment.

Feliz felt it throb and pulse and press against her thigh.

It was as though no time had passed.

Sway was speechless. He had never even considered touching another woman besides Charity from the day he laid eyes on her, This was not like him yet he felt this magnetic pull nearly akin to generous obligation when he looked up and saw Feliz's beautiful doe eyes gazing into his own.

His body seemed not to betray him, but rather to reveal it's truth. Sway's dick had never been so hard before and it throbbed for the touch of the woman in the yellow dress whose body was now pressed against his in the near dark. Sway's heart beat rapidly through his white oxford and he was suddenly unsure if he should have had that last glass of Armand De Brignac Rose.

"I have loved you so long, from so far." Sway's words dripped from his mouth with more truth than he had ever heard himself speak.

Joy flooded Feliz's soul, "I have wanted you every day, my whole life long. No one could ever replace you."

Their mouths met, and the thirst for each other led them into a deep kiss, his tongue flickering passionately across the underside of her perfectly pouty top lip.

It was as intoxicating as the first time, that night in the stair well on the way from the parking garage to the club.

She felt as though she could only belong everywhere he was, in all he did. She was nothing. She was everything.

Feliz was a part of this man, this twin soul, the depth of their connection frighteningly real. Each of their passion for the other both drowning and assuaging every fear, inhibition, wound. There was nothing between them, the two were bonded and unified in this mystery of relentless passion.

"I don't know what I'm doing." Sway plead the fifth for his entoxicatedness, and his open palm slid under her dress and around cupping her right ass cheek with strong tenderness in probing attention.

"Swallow me." He said in a husky whisper he had never heard from his own throat.

He backed her into the door she had just come out of, and it swung open.

To his odd dismay she reached behind him and dead bolted the door, The two of them ensued kissing passionately, thirstily, and he lifted the bottom half of her dress.

It was as though he was watching himself, and not himself, he knelt before her easing his tongue just below her navel, teasing her and plucking her panties to the side. He put them back in place and kissed her clit through them.

"I've wanted this for so long." She said, sounding as if she would cry and he hungrily tasted her until she lost all control. They were down on the floor like dirty beasts and her walls tightened around his tongue. Marcus could never touch her like this.

No man could.

"So you like calling people a lot and playing on their phone, is that it?" Swaynick McDaniels had officially arrived at the door to Feliz's soul.

He nibbled on her neck passionately. His manhood hard, and head dizzy from the Armand.

He knew the door was locked and he knew he was destined to passionately give this woman what her soul cried out for all those many years they were apart, him.

The shape of his magnificent penis was pressing through his slacks.

Sway went on, "I had asked you to behave."

He spoke with precision and strength in a hushed and gold glazed tone.

"You have the nerve to come here? Little girl, do you know what your doing?"

Sway glanced down noticing a tiny wet spot on his dark grey Tom Ford suit pants, Pre cum? He had not seen that since the last time they were together and he reached for the clasp on his Windsor base Sharkskin, his hand pressing and sliding beyond the boundary of Feliz's panty line into the warm wetness that was bubbling to welcome him home to her.

He removed his hand and mouth from hers only for a minute to unfasten and strip off his own pants and suddenly there was the sound of the door being rattled.

Fear flooded them both, Feliz there on the floor with her panties around her ankles, and Sway bottomless and hard as a diving board dangling in the air.

They were in a public place. What had just happened?

Sway was drunk and he didn't give a fuck.

He bent down to enter her hot whirlpool of candy coated passion and Feliz was still standing there in the mirror blinking her way back to reality. Sway was married now. She could choose to be happy about that for him, and that is what she did. The fantasy of them making love, fucking like horny animals in this restroom,

It was hers alone. Try as she might to send these telepathic snapshots of sexual energy and wantingness his way, it was her private fantasy. Now someone was at the door and she was being rude. Feliz had not touched herself but her mind had travelled into a realm of lustful whistfulness and bliss, was she crazy? Of course, but harmless, and she had too much respect for herself to laydown so easily for him. She needed reality to step in now from him,she had proved her love with her presence and she could only give him space now to persue her as she once had him. It was his turn.

Feliz was a woman who she knew she could get anyman, but she also knew she could not survive another heartbreak from this man, so she let all together fade the recounting of the lover's first time in a powerful HD, 3D replay full of improvisation, and whispers of love, she shook her head and pressed a cold wet paper towel onto her cheeks before she unlocked and opened the door.

This was her life now. She would never stop loving Sway from afar, she would never stop wanting him, but now she would never stop keeping him guessing as she gathered all of the strength and personal power she lost up and into herself like berries in her skirt, and she used it to remind herself that maybe one day the two of them would be different, in a different space and time, unhindered by their own lives and responsibilities, the daily grind and small consistent actions taken to put kids through school, keep partners laughing and smiling, keep bills paid, and not ruffle the norms, to honor the consistent, though sometimes boring, steady, colorfully drab consistentcies. washing her hands at the glass bowled modern sink, gazing into her own eyes and being. With the question, 'What must I do to get from this Universe to his?'

She shrugged and knowing that acceptance is the key to happiness she cried a single tear, wiped it away in one swipe and walked passed the woman walking in with her children leading her little boy to the bath stall.

It was time to go home, Marcus would be there asleep already no doubt and another day would come and go.

Swaynick was once again her intangible muse, Off limits in the real world.

Free to be with whomever he desired. Feliz could only be grateful she knew at least the fantasy of true love. There were no babies, no rich husbands, no million dollar checks coming in the mail but she was still beautiful, if not more now than ever and grateful, Sway was buggin and all of his celebrity homies were too.

He never even imagined there was another woman on earth who could own a room like his beautiful wife charity. Her laugh her smile her Essence the way she flit across the room like butterflies charity was a queen and everyone who encountered her knew it.

But this this woman, this creature in this yellow dress this was a magnetic goddess.

He needed a drink. He walked to the bar in an introverted disposition, doing his best to become invisible. It was Feliz, after all this time. She wore a yellow dress and Charity, though she did not know her saw her too.

Sway felt a surge of temptation but everyone knows black men don't cheat.

He wasn't about to even look like he was the type of man to go out like that.

"Bruh. NO ONE would blame you."

"All I know is she better stay her ass over there." And he swigged his cocktail glass of Brown sugar bourbon.

His boy Rick always seemed to pop up out of nowhere even still after all these years with the wrong advice.

Sway looked across the room at his lovely wife as she laughed with friends and put the yellow dressed goddess out of his mind.

Looking into her own eyes in the big luxury mirror before her, Feliz was starting to maybe get a glimpse of herself now, So she exited a side door at the High Museum while flashing back to the satisfaction of a sensually rewarding and creatively embellished memory of love, remembering her life before this moment when she had seen her light walking toward her on the street one fateful day so many years ago.

Her grandmother's wisdom echoing in her heart, that "Life is what you make it."

This was good. This was enough now. She only embraced Swaynick McDaniels in her heart remembering him now as just an ordinary man with a halo she once praised, accepting that because of her own issues, most of what she knew of him was an exhalted, airbrushed, high gloss version of him and likely not real at all. Feeling rejected by him invalidated her to her core and the only way she could take her power back now was to walk away with her chin held high while adjusting her own crown.

He had stood there in all of his prominence, having come so far from the point where she felt forced to let him go at two decades before, in his Tom Ford suit and gleaming wedding band, being a great host, greeting friends, and the air of this captivatingly beautiful but strange to her other woman 20 years later in Atlanta. She could only accept and admire.

Her grandfather told her, "You never miss the last bus."

And Feliz knew, there were far bigger fish. It was a joy seeing people were all together relieved having come out to this celebratory event for art music and mingling after having been quarantined indoors with some of them having recovered themselves, or lost loves ones but knowing they survived the deadliest viral contagion and pandemic the world had seen in a hundred years. Everyone felt beyond blessed to just be alive and well.

This extreme event had changed the lives of many truths were revealed, personal revelations were made homes were broken and founded, babies were made, and born, and whole churches and governments shut down. Millions of people died and the entire world was in a state of perpetual grief.

Feliz's missing one, Malina was a big head basic.

She got nearly 1 million Tik Tok views and you couldn't tell her nothin. She tried her best to keep everything simple to consistent fail as her own emotions often made the mess and she could not un-often get ahead every way she could. She was the girlfriend you would invite to the party to meet your man and she would devise a way to prove his disloyalty, dustiness, or worse just creep with him. She hated everyone and felt as though life owed her for her original misfortunes and she operated with an emptiness she often shrouded with a malicious conceit.

She heard she had a twin, another her, who had been abandoned in the trash bin with her all those years ago and she felt her absence and secretly prayed they would reunite so she would not have to feel so alone in the world. She was a powerhouse Leo/Virgo cusp with a *me against the world* shoulder chip the size of the Grand Canyon but everywhere she went she made sure beauty was her name.

Malina spent hours in the gym, weave stayed tight, hair done, nails done, everything did. She had already starred in 3 Hip hop music videos, and figured out how to retire from the pole by her 30th birthday.

Dangling the potential of fast sex was a means of getting whatever she wanted and her personal leverage for maneuvering in life.

Leverage.

Her needs were jumbled and sprinkled in with her life designed to serve her. She knew she was the shiny, fast car on the lot with her nas car curves and long natural hair flexing the Cape Verdean and Native American in her blood line. Life went her way every day except for not, that was until last year's physical.

She had some strange pain in her midsection and bleeding in her stool.

Her primary care sent her to a specialist and she was told her liver showed abnormalities. She knew it was from all the sauce over the years, living hard and fast on the club scene.

She was honestly shocked to be alive at all having witnessed the murder of two of the girls at the club.

They told her she needed a liver graft transplant to make it to her next birthday.

Malina was both dazed, devastated, and strangely relieved at the vague realty that she may not have to suffer this life anymore. Her whole life she had struggled with this morbid sense of impending doom. Often a storm cloud of despair always hung over her head just beneath the surface.

If only she knew her twin...she was determined to live her best life with all the time she had left.

This Thursday night she would do something different and go someplace she had never gone before...

Her Roberto Cavalli leopard safari leggings and Tigress caftan flattered her subtle curves and her long honey blonde highlighted tresses dangling down her back would not give her a liver graft from a matching donor but she would have fun!

She heard from a friend in her Lux life friend group on Facebook of this a new unmasking event complete with live music, art, and a slew of celebrity guests, from Deon Cole to Mary J Blige, LL Cool J and his beautiful wife Simone.

Pandemic have come in the last 2 years that rocked the nation and the world many died, infact Millions.

For the first time in her life thought the twin she's so longed for her entire life could have possibly died due to Corona virus and she wouldn't even know.

Elena gave up looking for her by the time she was 15 not knowing where to start except that their mother had disposed of them somewhere close to the West End.

But now is different now she needed her sister for her Liver graft transplant. She truly didn't want her life to be cut short with a fatal illness and this was the only one she knew for a fact would be a match so she did something she had stopped believing in for many years in her life for the first time in over a decade she prayed.

Only knew that if God was real and he was about all of the things they said he was about surely there would be hope for her somehow someway.

She turned around in her full length mirror fixing her hair ever so slightly looking back at it before she stepped out the door, "Girl chile if the Lord has made anything finer he could have kept it to himself. Wait maybe he did."

She left playfully and then traced down the hall toward her garage and drove away in her pearlescent Maserati.

Charity looked up from her conversation with the girls and noticed the woman she had seen earlier in the yellow dress but it looked like she changed clothes.

Charity summated that she was possibly a fashion model having a shoot at their event.

Sway was about to make a toast and Feliz was nowhere to be found which all though she trusted her husband was not disappointing to Charity.

As this beautiful melanin skinned soul walked out of the restroom post fantasizing about her long lost love she once briefly knew and held onto for dear life, she looked up at the walls leading back to the event space.

She noted the warm shadows the high hats shown giving variation to the space's energy.

Suddenly a stunningly attractive woman came around the corner wearing leopard pants and a tiger blouse.

She was classy and well dressed, shaped similar to Feliz…

Now the women caught their breath. It seemed standing before eachother, was the other…a plethora of emotions sprung upward to the surface.

Twins. United. Each of them sprung into tears and embraced.

There were no words, only a sigh a pause and another embrace.

Malina stammored, "I need you. I am sick...it›s my liver."

Immediately Feliz understood. It was in their sacred connection, the kind that only family has, the type of bond that far exceeds time and space.

"I am here."

Feliz resolved to keep her peace and sanity through it all by church services on the internet to make it through many lonely Sundays in her loft apartment downtown.

The pastor's word seared into her mind "Be with the one you cannot live without. Be with the one who adores & adorns you like the glory of sunflowers."

www.ingramcontent.com/pod-product-compliance
Lightning Source LLC
Chambersburg PA
CBHW031036190726
48286CB00003BA/1205